WITH HEARTFELT THANKS

Thank you, God, for using me and giving me the desires of my heart!!!!

Thank you to my husband, Dana, for your constant support of my dreams.

Big thanks to my mom, Freida, who encouraged me to always be better.

Thank you to all of my spiritual leaders for being the real deal, for walking in God's love, and for being great mentors who I can look up to.

Thank you to my professor, Mike Magoon, for helping me move forward with my ideas.

Thank you to my sister and best friend, Nicole, for always standing by my side and being there for me; your talent and creativity has always inspired me.

To my friends and sisters: Aunt Lori, Cousin Renee', Heather, Keri, Danielle, Lorene, Linda H., Alicia N., Jen A., and Michelle M.; thank you for all your support and loving me through it all!!!!

Thanks to Sharon Minard for the use of your beautiful cover photo.

Big thanks to my editor, Keri Stewart, for your constant support of my dreams!

Thanks to my four children Casey, Deanna, Dana jr., and Devon for teaching me how to survive parenting and the meaning of unconditional love.

Published by Michele West.
Printed in the USA.
First Printing, 2018.
Paperback ISBN: 978-1-5136-4307-6

This devotional is dedicated, first, to my daughters, Deanna and Casey. I love you both so much!

It's also dedicated to every woman of every age who is a Princess of God. We all are!

CONTENTS

Day 1

YOU'RE ENOUGH

. . . .

"Come to Me, all of you who work and have heavy loads. I will give you rest." Matthew 11:28 (NLV)

In the past, I always thought that I had to have the perfect husband, family, and kids. I went back to college for more schooling. I was always going after more and feeling it was never enough! Our God has taught me that I am enough in Him.

I was always trying to reinvent myself, because I wanted to be a woman of God. My husband was first priority followed by my kids. I tried to juggle it all.

I had several different gifts. My husband says that I'm a Renaissance woman. Let God lead your life and trust Him in your life whether you're a stay-at-home mom, which is a full-time, 24/7 job, or a CEO of a company, or a janitor at a school.

There is nothing wrong with learning more or bettering yourself, but make sure you check with God first. Make sure it's not you, but He, who is leading you.

Day 2

YOU'RE LOVED

....

"God so loved the world that He gave His only begotten Son." John 3:16

Our God loves you so much! It's hard to wrap our brains around a Father's Love with no strings attached.

There's nothing you could do or not do to make Him love you any less!

Day 3

FAITH

. . . .

"Faith does not make things easy. It makes them possible." Luke 1:37

I learned about Faith at 20 years old. Faith is the substance of things unseen. You're told to have Faith the size of a mustard seed, and it can carry you through!

I learned some different teachings on Faith in my 40s. I know I am a woman of Faith. There was a time where my health declined so terribly. I held onto my Faith and Jesus. That's all you have when you're faced with any horrific situation. Faith is simple: it's believing that God can and that you can't.

Regarding having the Faith to be healed: It's not due to lack of Faith that you don't receive. Don't ever believe anyone who says that you're sick as a result of too little Faith. That's not the Word of God. Adam and Eve fell in the garden. Everything came into our world then. God does have the power to heal, but sometimes, He doesn't bring healing. We must focus on His Will, not ours.

I overcame that season in victory in Christ. It seemed as if it would never end, but our God is a big God, and He will carry you through anything. Have faith to go to doctors, and pray on the way there. God loves you! And He will use this time to glorify Himself.

Day 4

HE'S GOT THIS

"Trust in the Lord with all your heart, and lean not on your own understanding. In all your ways, acknowledge Him, and He will make your paths straight."
Proverbs 3:5-6

Ever feel like, "Wow. What now God?!"

God brings things into our lives to mold us and stretch us beyond our comfort zones. I know this all too well. If we are comfortable, we're really not growing.

I find myself in situations that leave me thinking, "Wow, Lord. How can I be used here?" or "Lord, this is too much." No. God says that He's enough. And if we give it to Him and have His Holy Spirit live and dwell within us, we have the power to help anyone!

Proverbs 3:5-6 is my all-time favorite scripture. I realized in my 30s that the Holy Spirit lives within me and that I don't need to be afraid of what life brings me. You're equipped with Christ within you.

Trust Him in your trials, situations, daily life, work, children, and location. He's got this! Daily, hand things over to Him, and thank Him!

Day 5

EVERY DAY IS A GIFT

. . . .

"You can do all things through Christ who strengthens you!" Philippians 4:13

I wake up at the crack of dawn each day. Early to bed. Early to rise! I wake up with an excitement that it's a new day. Sometimes I feel like a kid on Christmas morning!

I know you're probably saying, "What's up with her?" I do love my coffee!

There was a time when I couldn't just jump up and start my day. I prayed long, had Faith, and went to church. People laid hands on me. I listened to worship music and read the Word.

When you go through something that almost takes you from this world, you have a grateful heart more than ever before. You're forever changed and transformed like never before!

My favorite quote that I live by is this: "Yesterday is history. Tomorrow is a mystery. Today is a gift of God, which is why we call it the 'present'."

Day 6

JOY

. . . .

"The Joy of the Lord is our strength." Nehemiah 8:10
"Fill my heart with greater Joy." Psalm 4:7

An attitude of gratitude promotes Joy! A thankful heart is a happy heart. Joy is more than happiness. Joy is the Holy Spirit within us that doesn't blow away like leaves. Joy is deep within us. It is something that no one can take away!

Day 7

A FATHER'S LOVE

. . . .

"He is a Father to the fatherless." Psalm 68:5

"No one comes to the Father except through Me." John 14:6

"Honor your father and mother." Exodus 20:12

"God will never love you any less." Romans 8:14

Even if you grew up not knowing your earthly father, Jesus says in His Word, in Deuteronomy 32:10, that we are the apple of His eye. As a parent, I feel just like this about my own children. We are children of God. A Father's Love is unconditional!

I say this often, because I know it now. There is nothing we can do to make Him love us any more or any less. We are His creation first; then He sends us down to earthly parents.

Day 8

TRUST IN HIM

. . . .

"It is better to trust in the Lord than to put confidence in man." Psalm 118:8 (NKJV)

Trusting in the Lord is not natural for most people. This Princess of God devotional is an exercise in discipline, letting go, stepping out of us, and trusting in Him!

God has allowed so many things in my life to happen so that I would have a desperation for Him and nothing else and so that I would trust Him. It wasn't until I began to fully surrender and trust him that my life changed.

Don't put your trust in people, place, and things. Put your trust in the Lord.

Day 9

GOD MADE YOU A LEADER

"I call to you from the end of the earth when my heart is weak. Lead me to the rock that is higher than I."
Psalm 61:2

I definitely was a born leader. I'm the oldest of 3 siblings. Everything in this world says I should have been a follower according to my upbringing. But God had other plans! I am so grateful!

Being a leader means being obedient to our true leader, Jesus Christ. We can do nothing of ourselves. Believe me. I know firsthand. The Lord loved me so much that He allowed me to go as far as I could with my own will until one day, I was leveled and surrendered completely to His direction, leadership, guidance, everything! I never looked back. I knew I had found strength from Him, not from me.

Day 10

BE HEALED

....

"But He was hurt for our wrong-doing. He was crushed
for our sins. He was punished so we would have peace.
He was beaten so we would be healed."
Isaiah 53:5 (NLV)

The Word says, "By Your stripes, we are healed." Jesus did take it all on the cross for us. Be healed physically, emotionally, mentally, and spiritually.

We do have Faith to exercise in these areas of our lives to be whole. The Lord said that in this life, there will be many trials. Let me make one thing clear: you can have faith to move mountains; you can have great faith. And God can still, sometimes, say, "No." This is not a reflection of your lack of faith. I see different churches practicing this idea of Faith, but it is not life-giving. It actually is death and condemnation to most people.

You are a child of God, and with what He's equipped you with, you do the very best you can in life. He will see you through.

Day 11

EXTENDED LOVE & GRACE

"*Follow God's example, therefore, as dearly loved children and was in the way of love, just as Christ loved us and gave himself up for us as a fragrant offering and sacrifice to God.*" Ephesians 5:1

I know this one oh-so-well: Extended Love. We give to unlovely people, people in our world whom God has put there to love on even if they are the most unlovely. I see this over and over in my life. We need to give extended love to those whom no one would even talk to!

Extended Grace: I have received this myself. Love people where they're at. Don't be a doormat, but love them and extend Grace their way. You might be the only Jesus they see!

This truly has been an exercise of discipline for me through the years.

Ephesians 5 says that when we walk in Love, we are abiding as imitators of God, as dear children. We are walking in Love as Christ also has Loved us and given Himself for us.

Day 12

BE REAL

. . . .

"We are careful to be honorable before the Lord, but we also want everyone else to see that we are honorable."
2 Corinthians 8:21

One of the greatest lessons I've learned in life is to be real and transparent!

People either love your transparency, or they are afraid of it. It is a blessing to me. I believe that when much is given, much is required. Jesus has some of us remain transparent so that others can see that the Love of God is for them and be healed.

Let the walls down and become transparent, so others can receive God's Love. Be real to others! As my husband always says, "You've got to give it away to keep it!"

Day 13

FEAR OF THE LORD

. . . .

"The fear of the Lord is the beginning of wisdom, and knowledge of the Holy One is understanding."
Proverbs 9:10

Fear of the Lord really means to depart from all evil. We are all works in progress. We are blessed to wake up every day and have a fresh start with Him. Every day is a new day in which we can choose to reject the lies of the enemy, and dig into God's Word, and let it be branded on our hearts and minds.

Day 14

LET YOUR LIGHT SHINE

"Let your light shine before others, that they may see your good deeds and glorify your Father in Heaven."
Matthew 5:16

In this world, choose every day when you wake up, even before coffee: I'm going to let my light shine at school, at work, at the supermarket, everywhere. It's all about choices and a thankful heart! You can shine a light in almost every situation.

The Lord tells us many times to be light in a dark world. People need to see light in us daily. It's Hope. It's Joy. It's Love. It's Spirit led.

Day 15

ABIDE

. . . .

"Remain in me, as I also remain in you. No branch can bear fruit by itself; it must remain in the vine. Neither can you bear fruit unless you remain in me."
John 15:4

"If you keep my commands, you will remain in my love, just as I have kept my Father's commands and remain in his love." John 15:10

Abiding in Christ is simply obedience. Ouch. This one is hard but not if you are being led by His Spirit and exercising it daily.

One of my daughters is now 20 years old. She's an amazing young lady of God. She goes to college, serves at her church, and encourages others. She recently got a tattoo with the word "Abide" on her inner arm. This is the child who flipped out when getting her ears pierced or a flu shot! How did she do this?

She, like all of us, needed a constant reminder to obey God no matter what.

Day 16

BE OBEDIENT

"Then he took the Book of the Covenant and read it to the people. They responded, 'We will do everything the Lord has said; we will obey.'" Exodus 24:7

"Do not conform to the pattern of this world, but be transformed by the renewing of your mind. Then you will be able to test and approve what God's will is – his good, pleasing and perfect will." Romans 12:2

The single, most important key to knowing the Father's will for us is to obey Him, no matter what's happening in life. You have to renew your mind in Christ. This causes obedience. Read His word, believing in your heart first, then your head. God's word is life transformation, and when you do this, you're being obedient.

Day 17

SURRENDER YOUR HEART

"Yet if you devote your heart to him and stretch out. Your hands to him, if you put away the sin that is in your hand and allow no evil to dwell in your tent, then, free of fault, you will lift up your face; you sill stand firm and without fear." Job 11:13-15

This one was a tough one for me. I grew up without a father's love. Men came in and out of my life as a child.

Surrendering to Christ means finally realizing that nothing else such as a job, money, clothing, people, cars, vacations, the gym, etc can fulfill you. When you know there has to be more, then you are ready to surrender your heart.

I was 20 years old when I gave my life to Christ. Boy, did He have His work cut out! It was the best decision of my life! I thank Him daily for loving me, forgiving me, being there for me, filling me, and carrying me. Struggling to surrender fully to God is a heart issue based on lack of trust.

Knowledge is in your head, but everything flows from the heart. You need to be born again to have renewal of the mind. This begins within the heart first.

Day 18

IT'S ALL ABOUT THE HEART

. . . .

"Therefore, if anyone is in Christ, the new creation has come: The old has gone. The new is here!" 2 Corinthians 5:17

Everything that comes from your mouth begins within the heart. God has healed me of heart wounds. I choose every day to be a better version of myself, because Christ is within me. We have a lot to be grateful for. With Christ in me, I'm a new creation. Old things are passed away, and all things are made new.

Day 19

HEAD KNOWLEDGE

....

"I will think about Your Law and have respect for Your ways." Isaiah 53:5 (NLV)

You can have all the head knowledge in the world and be no earthly good. Yikes! It is great to study, earn a degree, and reach that goal. But make sure that God is your firm foundation. It's not about us and our achievements; It's all about Him.

Day 20

GOD'S OWN HEART

"For as the heavens are higher than the earth, so are My ways higher than your ways, and My thoughts than your thoughts." Isaiah 55:9 (NLV)

Chasing after God's own heart is not always easy. Things of this world are not God's own.

We go day after day as Christians who are trying to be like God's own heart. The key is prayer and time with Him first thing each day. We need to get rid of hang-ups and sinful behaviors. Even if you're blind to them, ask God to reveal His heart to you so that you can be at peace in this world.

Day 21

DAILY HEART CHECK

. . . .

"Above all else, guard your heart, for everything you do flows from it." Proverbs 4:23

My time for me and God is when I first wake up and everyone else is still sleeping. I start by doing my daily inventory, my "heart check". I ask God to remove anything from within me that is not right. I learned to do this many years ago but found that, with life's ups and downs, I needed to be on my game and check my heart daily. This, at first, was a discipline. It made me surrender more to Him and get brutally honest with myself and with God.

It's not that we are terrible people. We are all sinners, and without doing daily heart checks, we can become much like the world for whom we're supposed to be lights.

A daily heart check prepares us for our day. There's freedom in letting go... to the Lord, and Joy follows that!

Day 22

VICTORIOUS LIVING

"I press on toward the goal to win the prize for which God has called me heavenward in Christ Jesus."
Philippians 3:14

Living in victory is very freeing! It's making a daily choice to not let people, places, and things rob you of your Joy. Victorious living does not come from our own strength. It comes from choosing to give over to God the cares of our world, and move forward no matter how that might look. That's victorious living!

Day 23

OVERCOMING THE FIERY DARTS

"Peace I leave with you. My peace I give you. I do not give to you as the world gives. Do not let your hearts be troubled and do not be afraid." John 14:27

In life, you'll endure many trials. I have seen many in my 46 years. I honestly never went through one alone. Thank you, Lord! You can choose to let the fiery darts penetrate or bounce off of you. This took a little time for me and was a process. Handing things over more and more to God was such a better choice than letting myself endure everyone else's whim or upset.

God has given me a strength I have never known, and I trust Him with my everything. I'm nothing without Him, and I'm everything with Him.

Day 24

PEACE, LOVE, & HOPE

"May the God of hope fill you with all joy and peace as you trust in him, so that you may overflow with hope by the power of the Holy Spirit." Romans 15:13

God comes to us to reveal his peace, love, and hope so that we might live a life second to none. God is a Hope to carry on peace to calm any storm and a Love to refresh and endure forever!

Day 25

GOD-BUILT

"Anyone who listens to my teaching and follows it is wise, like a person who builds a house on solid rock. Though the rain comes in torrents and the floodwaters rise and the winds beat against that house, it won't collapse because it is built on bedrock. But anyone who hears my teaching and doesn't obey it is foolish, like a person who builds a house on sand. When the rains and floods come and the winds beat against that house, it will collapse with a mighty crash."
Matthew 7:24-27 (NLT)

I had an idea for a story years ago about how God lays the foundation of our life when we surrender to Him. Our building history is our family. I love to see the layers of foundation that God has laid out for us to be successful projects in Christ.

I'm so glad that God has freed me from all control and that I let Him lead and build the foundations of my life. You can do this too! His ways are so much better than ours!

Day 26

YOU NEVER LET GO

"And surely I am with you always, to the very end of the age." Matthew 28:20

I thank God every day for his unconditional Love for me. No matter how much I do right or wrong, He'll never let go! We are all trying to be the best version of ourselves with His help, right? I wake up every morning with Him on my mind first so that I spend the day with Him thanking Him for everything. He'll never let go just like the song says:

"Oh no, you never let go

Through the calm and through the storm

Oh no, you never let go

Every high and every low

Oh no, you never let go

Lord, You never let go of me!"

He's so awesome and worthy to be praised!

Day 27

FREE

. . . .

"He heals the brokenhearted and binds up their wounds." Psalm 147:3

"Jesus looked at them and said, 'With man this is impossible, but with God all things are possible.'" Matthew 19:26

As I grew older, I understood more of what it meant to be free: free in Christ. God had to heal old wounds and set this girl free. It didn't happen overnight. There was a lot to undo. The process was sometimes heart wrenching, exhausting, confusing, and lonely.

God has turned those things around and healed me in my deepest core with his forgiveness, patience, grace, love, and mercy for me. He can do the same for you if you let Him. When you are going through a healing process, it's definitely not for the weak. You are strong

in Him, and He will see you through every step of the
way!

Day 28

EVERY DAY IS A NEW DAY

....

"This is the day the Lord has made; We will rejoice and be glad in it." Psalm 118:24 (NKJV)

I go to bed at night thanking God for all things and what He's done in my life. I go to sleep pretty quickly, wake up refreshed, and thank Him again for the new day. His mercies are new every morning. We have a chance every day to become more like Him.

Day 29

LET GOD LEAD YOU

"The Lord will always lead you. He will meet the needs of your soul in the dry times and give strength to your body. You will be like a garden that has enough water, like a well of water that never dries up." Isaiah 58:11 (NLV)

Those who walk with God will always reach their destination. I've learned through the years to trust Him more and more through my walk with Him. Trust was a big thing for me since I was a young teen. Our God is so gentle, and if we ask for understanding and for Him to reveal himself in a way that we can see Him, He does. We can trust Him with everything.

I remember worrying about different things that were out of my control asking God, "How do I do this?" or "How do I prepare for this?" I would ask a lot of questions. I would see the Lord saying, "Yes, dear. What do you have for me today?" God has shown me dozens of times that I could completely trust Him and give Him my life and my everything. I'll let Him lead. I'm free.

Pray to release full control to God's leading daily.

Day 30

BEING A PRINCESS OF GOD

. . . .

"'For I know the plans I have for you,' says the Lord, 'plans for well-being and not for trouble, to give you a future and a hope.'" Jeremiah 29:11 (NLV)

"With God all things are possible." Matthew 19:26

For me, it took years to understand my Father in Heaven's Love for me. I do know it now, and you can too. Being a Princess of God is not about being perfect or beautiful. It's not about your income or status. It's simply about being a daughter and resting in the arms of Christ.

Whether you're a student, stay at home mom, cashier, CEO, or barista, it's all good. We need to know that our value comes from Him and not from what we do.

ABOUT THE AUTHOR

Michele West, is a 46-year-young mother of 4 who has been happily married to her husband, Dana, for 25 years. She has worked with and mentored women of all ages for the past two decades. She finds joy in helping women find their true worth in God and Jesus and realize all that they can be in and through Him.

Michele is a very creative woman with many gifts. She has co-written a number of worship songs with her husband Dana. In addition to Princess of God 30 Day Devotional, she plans to write children's stories, ministry books, and novels. Michele is also an entrepreneur and has plans to launch new products.

One of her goals is to encourage women to find the gifts that God has for them.

Michele has a heart for women of all ages. During her young adult life, she modeled and worked for a major Boston Radio station. As a result, she has gained wisdom to share with young women seeking to navigate paths in an often-treacherous industry. She has overcome fear, trust issues, rejection, and disappointment. Michele's testimony is an amazing story of trusting in God and persevering with His help. She is truly a miracle and has experienced many physical healings in her life, including a miraculous healing during surgery.

Michele feels that all of this was preparation from God for her time now. Her desire is to share the transforming power of God she has experienced in her life and help others discover their purpose and value in Jesus!

Michele is available to come to your church to speak, teach, and share her testimony for a love offering.